D0251169

The LAST FIREHAWK

The Shadowlands

by
Katrina Charman

BRANCHES™

SCHOLASTIC INC.

The LAST FIREHAWK

Read All the Books

1. The LAST FIREHAWK — The Ember Stone
2. The LAST FIREHAWK — The Crystal Caverns
3. The LAST FIREHAWK — The Whispering Oak
4. The LAST FIREHAWK — Lullaby Lake
5. The LAST FIREHAWK — The Shadowlands
6. The LAST FIREHAWK — The Battle for Perodia
7. The LAST FIREHAWK — The Cloud Kingdom

Table of Contents

Introduction 1

Map 2

Chapter 1: The Final Journey 4

Chapter 2: Enemies 9

Chapter 3: Into the Shadowlands 14

Chapter 4: The March 20

Chapter 5: Thorn's Army 25

Chapter 6: Wolves 28

Chapter 7: Trapped! 34

Chapter 8: The Missing Sack 40

Chapter 9: Rumble Underground 45

Chapter 10: In the Tunnels 50

Chapter 11: To Valor Wood 56

Chapter 12: Home 62

Chapter 13: The Last Piece 68

Chapter 14: The Golden Feather 73

Chapter 15: Grey's Tree 77

Chapter 16: Grey's Army 85

For Maddie, Piper, and Riley. –KC

Library of Congress Cataloging-in-Publication Data

Names: Charman, Katrina, author. | Norton, Jeremy, illustrator. | Charman, Katrina. Last firehawk ; 5.
Title: The Shadowlands / by Katrina Charman ; illustrated by Jeremy Norton.
Description: First edition. | New York : Branches/Scholastic Inc., 2019. |
Series: The last firehawk ; 5 | Summary: Tag the owl, Skyla the squirrel, and Blaze the firehawk are searching for the final piece of the magical Ember Stone that will hopefully save Perodia from the evil vulture Thorn, and their quest has led them to the Howling Caves in Valor Wood—but they do not know if the stone will actually be there, or what will be waiting for them when they emerge into the spreading darkness.
Identifiers: LCCN 2018011089 | ISBN 9781338307115 (pbk : alk. paper) |
ISBN 9781338307122 (hjk : alk. paper)
Subjects: LCSH: Owls—Juvenile fiction. | Squirrels—Juvenile fiction. |
Animals, Mythical—Juvenile fiction. | Quests (Expeditions)—Juvenile fiction. | Magic—Juvenile fiction. | Adventure stories. | CYAC:
Owls—Fiction. | Squirrels—Fiction. | Animals, Mythical—Fiction |
Magic—Fiction. | Adventure and adventurers—Fiction. | Fantasy. | LCGFT:
Action and adventure fiction.
Classification: LCC PZ7.1.C495 Sh 2019 | DDC [Fic]—dc23 LC record available at https://lccn.loc.gov/2018011089

10 9 8 7 6 5 4 3 2 1   19 20 21 22 23

Printed in China   62

First edition, February 2019
Illustrated by Judit Tondora
Edited by Katie Carella
Book design by Maria Mercado

⌐ INTRODUCTION ⌐

In the enchanted land of Perodia,
lies Valor Wood—a forest filled with magic and
light. There, a wise owl named Grey leads the
Owls of Valor. These brave warriors protect
the creatures of the wood. But a darkness is
spreading across Perodia, and the forest's magic
and light are fading away . . .

A powerful old vulture called Thorn controls
The Shadow—a dark magic. Whenever The
Shadow appears, Thorn and his army of orange-
eyed spies are nearby. Thorn will not stop until
Perodia is destroyed.

Tag, a small barn owl, and his friends Skyla
and the last firehawk, Blaze, have found four pieces
of the magical Ember Stone. This stone holds a
powerful magic that may be bright enough to stop
Thorn once and for all. But there is one more piece
to be found before the stone is complete. Thorn
and his spies are closing in fast. Tag's journey
continues . . .

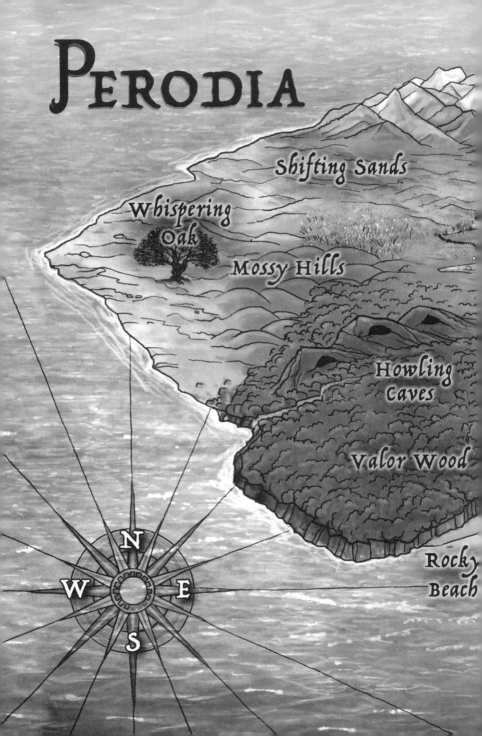

THE FINAL JOURNEY

Tag watched the ground whiz by below as he flapped his wings as hard as he could. His best friends raced through the air beside him. Skyla was on Blaze's back. And Blaze, with her huge gold, red, and orange wings, soared through the sky.

Skyla called out to Tag, but he couldn't hear her over the rushing wind. He pointed to the ground.

Tag landed with a soft bump. Blaze landed beside him and Skyla hopped down.

"Are we going the right way?" Skyla asked. "I thought we'd be flying farther north."

Blaze gave a small peep. She looked worried.

"Let's check the map," Tag said.

First, he looked around. There was no sign of Thorn or his orange-eyed spies. The sky was sunny and clear.

Next, Tag reached into his sack and pulled out the magical map. He unfolded it and pointed to where they were, near Lullaby Lake.

Then Blaze pointed to where they were headed: Valor Wood.

"We need to get to Valor Wood quickly and find the last missing piece of the Ember Stone," Tag said. "It won't be long before Thorn and The Shadow find us."

Skyla frowned. "But if we keep going in this direction, we'll fly right over Thorn's home—The Shadowlands."

"We should not cross The Shadowlands!" Blaze cried.

Tag patted her wing. "I know you are scared, Blaze," he said. "I am, too, but we need to take the quickest path. We are so close to defeating Thorn once and for all."

"But what if Thorn's spies see us flying over The Shadowlands?" Skyla asked. Her tail was twitching back and forth. "There are so many of them! We can't fight them all."

Tag pointed at the map. "We'll only fly over this top corner of The Shadowlands."

"As long as we fly fast," Tag added, "we'll cross it in no time. Then we will be safe in Valor Wood with Grey and the Owls of Valor."

Skyla looked at Blaze and Tag, then sighed. "You're both going to have to fly faster than you have ever flown before," she said.

"I'm ready!" Blaze said with a nod.

Tag opened his wings, and the friends set off toward The Shadowlands.

ENEMIES

The friends flew on. Tag felt the air grow colder. He could see The Shadowlands up ahead.

As they reached the edge of Thorn's home, the midday sun moved behind some gray clouds and the sky above went dark. There was no sign of light or of the clear blue sky. It was almost as black as night.

Tag shivered. "I guess now we know why this part of Perodia is called The Shadowlands," he called to his friends.

"I don't like the look of this one bit," Skyla added. "It's so creepy."

Tag and Blaze flapped their wings harder.

Below, the land was grey and dusty. There was no color at all. The only plants Tag could see were dead trees and thick, twisty bushes with thorns as long and sharp as a tiger bat's beak.

"We're almost across!" Tag yelled to his friends.

With her long wings, Blaze could fly much faster than Tag. Usually she flew beside him, but The Shadowlands had scared them all and she started to fly ahead. Skyla held on tight, trying not to look down.

"Hurry, Tag!" Skyla called behind her.

Tag focused ahead. He could see the sun again, peeping out along the edge of Valor Wood. He flew faster and caught up to Blaze.

But in the sky, at the far edge of The Shadowlands, was a dark, fuzzy cloud. And it was heading right for them.

What is that? Tag wondered. He narrowed his eyes, trying to see the cloud more clearly. Soon, Tag realized it wasn't a cloud after all. It was glowing. He gasped. *Thorn's spies!*

"We have to turn back!" Tag shouted.

Hundreds of tiny orange eyes sped toward them.

"Locusts!" Blaze yelled over the buzz of the flying creatures.

Tag squinted. The locusts were small and green with clear wings. *They look like flying grasshoppers, but grasshoppers are friendly creatures,* Tag thought. *These locusts are not.*

"We've flown so far already!" Skyla cried. "We can't go backward!"

"Where else can we go?" Blaze asked.

Tag glanced down at the thornbushes below. There was only one choice.

"We have to get out of the sky," he said as the locusts zoomed toward them. "Into The Shadowlands!"

INTO THE SHADOWLANDS

The three friends landed in the Shadowlands with a bump. Tag managed to miss a prickly thornbush, but Blaze and Skyla crash-landed right in the middle of one.

"Skyla! Blaze!" Tag called. "Are you okay?"

Blaze hopped out of the bush, licking her
wings. Skyla tried to follow, but—

"My tail is stuck!" she cried.

In the sky, the locusts were circling like a
big, buzzing cloud.

The friends had to move fast.

Tag and Blaze tugged at Skyla's thick,
bushy tail. Finally, it came free, and she
tumbled to the ground.

The buzzing sound above grew louder.

Blaze looked up at the sky. "The locusts are going to attack!" she said.

The locusts began to dive. They were aiming right at them.

Skyla pulled out her slingshot and Tag gripped his golden dagger, but Blaze stepped in front of them both.

SKRAAAAAAAAAAAAAAA!

Tag and Skyla covered their ears as Blaze
let out her firehawk cry.

The cloud of locusts exploded as the
creatures scattered in different directions.

"You did it, Blaze!" Tag cried. "Your
powerful cry scared them off!"

The friends hugged.

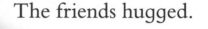

Then Skyla jumped onto Blaze's back.

"We need to get out of here," she said.
"Those locusts will tell Thorn where we are.
More spies will be here soon!"

Tag nodded. He quickly checked his sack to make sure that their piece of the Ember Stone was safe. Then he spread his wings.

"Let's go!" he said.

But Skyla and Blaze did not move. They stared at the sky. Their fur and feathers were shaking.

Tag looked up. Darker than any storm cloud and scarier than any of Thorn's spies was . . . The Shadow.

THE MARCH

The Shadow became darker and darker. It filled the sky.

Tag could see flashes of lightning within The Shadow. "We can't fly now," he said. "The Shadow destroys everything it touches."

"What are we going to do?" Skyla asked.

"We will have to make our way out of The Shadowlands on foot," Tag said.

Another noise filled the air. Loud squawks and snapping beaks.

"Tiger bats!" Blaze cried.

"They are not alone," Tag said. Locusts were flying beneath The Shadow, among the orange-eyed tiger bats.

"The locusts must have already told Thorn we are here," Skyla said. "We need to hide. Now!"

The friends ran as fast as they could, staying close to the thorny bushes and beneath the twisting, dead trees.

Tag could hear a strange marching sound in the distance.

"In here!" Blaze shouted.

Tag and Skyla followed Blaze to a huge old tree. Tag took off his sack and the friends squeezed into a hole in the bottom of its hollow trunk.

The ground seemed to rumble as the marching sound came closer.

"Quick! Climb up into the tree," Tag said. "If Thorn's spies are on the ground, they could spot us hiding in this opening."

Blaze climbed up inside the tree. Skyla quickly followed, with Tag behind her. They climbed up as far as they could.

The marching sound was now very loud.

Tag peeked out through a small hole in the tree.

"What is that noise?" Skyla whispered. "Can you see anything, Tag?"

Tag peered down out of the tree hole. It looked like the ground was moving—like a red-and-black river was flowing across the land. But it wasn't water. It was thousands of tiny prickle ants and crag beetles. They marched together.

"I see more of Thorn's spies! There's an army of prickle ants and crag beetles outside! And it looks like they are all headed for the same place," he said. Tag looked into the distance. "They're marching toward Valor Wood!"

THORN'S ARMY

"We need to warn Grey that Thorn's spies are headed to Valor Wood!" Skyla said. "We need to get out of here!"

Tag shook his head. There was nowhere for them to go—not as long as the march of spies was right outside the tree.

"We need to wait," Blaze agreed.

Tag watched the prickle ants and crag beetles march past.

"What are prickle ants and crag beetles doing in The Shadowlands anyway?" Skyla asked.

"I don't know," Tag replied.

The last time they had seen the biting red prickle ants was in Valor Wood. And they had run into the crag beetles near the Whispering Oak.

"It looks like Thorn has called all his spies to The Shadowlands—or to Valor Wood," Tag guessed.

What is Thorn planning? he wondered.

After a while, Tag peeked out of the tree hole again. "The army is gone," he told Skyla and Blaze.

"But the tiger bats and locusts could still be in the sky searching for us," Skyla warned. "And I'm sure The Shadow is still overhead."

"We cannot wait any longer," Blaze said. "It's time."

"Follow me," Tag agreed, climbing down inside the tree trunk. "Stay close to the bushes and trees so we won't be seen."

The friends hurried away from the tree.

Tag glanced up at the sky. Sure enough, the tiger bats were still circling above. Tag held his sack tight.

All of a sudden, he bumped into something furry and very, very big!

WOLVES

Tag stared up at two very large, hungry-looking wolves. Blaze peeped as Skyla pulled out her slingshot. Tag quickly hid the sack behind his back as the three friends huddled together.

The wolves had long, black claws and sharp teeth. One was white and one was gray. Their eyes glowed orange. The gray wolf growled.

GRRRRRRRRRRRR!

Tag stumbled, dropping his sack on the ground.

He turned to grab it. But the sack was gone!

Where did my sack go? Tag wondered. He looked at Blaze. The firehawk was staring at a pile of dirt behind him, her eyes wide.

The wolves growled again, and the friends all turned to face them.

"Well, well," the white wolf said. "Look who we found."

Skyla's paws shook as she held out her slingshot. "Stay back!" she cried.

The gray wolf laughed. "Or what?"

"I'll—" Before Skyla could say any more, the white wolf had grabbed her slingshot in his jaws. He threw it into the closest bush.

"Give us the Ember Stone!" the white wolf ordered, sniffing at their armor, searching for the stone.

"We don't have it," Tag said.

"He's telling the truth," the gray wolf said.

"They are no use to us without the stone," the white wolf growled. "Let's take them to the cages."

"Blaze," Tag whispered. "Use your cry!"

Blaze opened her beak, ready to scare the wolves away. But the two wolves were fast! In a blur, they were right behind Tag and Skyla. So close that Tag could feel their breath on his feathers. They snapped their jaws and growled louder than before.

"Keep your beak shut," the white wolf snarled at Blaze, "or we'll hurt your friends."

Blaze closed her beak.

"Thorn won't be happy when we tell him we don't have the Ember Stone," the gray wolf whispered to the white one.

The white wolf looked at Blaze. "At least we have the firehawk," he said. "She's worth something to Thorn."

"What about the other two?" the gray wolf asked.

The white wolf snarled. "We will make sure they are out of Thorn's way for good."

TRAPPED!

Tag gulped and looked at his friends. Skyla's eyes were wide with fear. But Blaze looked angry.

Blaze stamped her feet. She ran at the wolves before her friends could stop her. The wolves leaped aside.

"Use your firepower!" Skyla called.

Blaze narrowed her eyes. Her feathers began to light up, one by one, glowing with red, gold, and orange flames. The wolves backed away, watching her bright wings.

Tag pulled out his dagger and grabbed Skyla's slingshot from the nearby bush. He tossed it to her.

Skyla shot acorns at the wolves' heads, but the acorns bounced off their fur.

Blaze shot a fireball at the wolves, but it hit the wolves' fur and then exploded on the ground. The wolves laughed.

"Firehawks are not the only creatures with magical powers," the white wolf said. "Our fur is thicker than any armor—and it's fireproof! That's why Thorn sent *us* to find you."

"And you are not the only ones with magical friends," the gray wolf added. He looked up and shouted: "Spiders!"

A big, hairy, black creature dropped suddenly from a branch above. Another spider followed, then another.

Skyla shrieked as a spider crawled over her. The eight-legged creature quickly tied her paws together with its web.

Another did the same to Tag so he could not move his wings.

Blaze tried to use her powerful cry, but the orange-eyed spider was faster. It spun a thick, silver web around Blaze's beak and wings.

The gray wolf grinned. "You are in The Shadowlands now," he said. "Thorn's spies are everywhere. You will never escape."

The white wolf took Tag's and Skyla's weapons. Then they pushed the three friends through the forest of dead trees, deeper into The Shadowlands.

"Tag," Skyla whispered as they trudged along, "where is the Ember Stone?"

Tag shook his head. He looked back, trying to figure out what might have happened to his sack. Blaze tried to tell him something by pointing her beak at the ground.

"I don't understand," Tag said.

"Be quiet!" the gray wolf growled.

The group arrived at two large cages. They were made from dead tree branches and twisted together with thick vines. The wolves pushed Skyla and Tag into one cage and Blaze into the other.

The white wolf tossed the friends' weapons aside.

"Welcome to your new home," the gray wolf snarled.

THE MISSING SACK

The wolves guarded the cages, walking in circles around them.

Tag lowered his head. The Ember Stone was lost, they were trapped in cages, the wolves had their weapons, and worst of all— Thorn would take Blaze away and use her for her magical powers.

"There's no way out," he said.

Skyla shook her head. "Don't give up, Tag. There must be a way!"

Tag sighed. "I have let everyone down," he said. "This is all my fault. I should have listened to you both. We should have stayed away from The Shadowlands."

BA-WAAAA! BA-WAAAA!

A loud horn sound filled the air. The wolves' ears pricked up.

"Thorn is calling. We need to go," said the white wolf.

"What about our prisoners?" said the gray wolf.

The white wolf looked at the caged friends. "Those three won't be going anywhere," he growled. "Just think how happy Thorn will be when we tell him we have captured the last firehawk!"

The wolves laughed as they ran off in the same direction as the march of spies.

"We need to get free and find my sack!" Tag said. He used his beak to break the web tying Skyla's paws together.

"Where did the sack go? What happened to it?" Skyla asked, working on Tag's wings.

"I hid it behind my back to keep the wolves from seeing it, but then I dropped it," Tag said, pulling the web from his wings. "When I turned around, it was gone."

Blaze stomped inside her cage, trying to tell Tag something.

"Don't worry, Blaze," Tag called out to his friend. "We'll find a way out of this somehow."

Skyla pulled at the thick vines that tied the wooden cages together. "We have to hurry," she said. "We can't let Thorn take Blaze."

Tag helped Skyla, using his beak, but it was no use. The vines were too strong.

He sat on the ground with a sigh. *If only I had my dagger*, he thought.

Suddenly, there was a rumble beneath him. The earth began to shake.

RUMBLE
UNDERGROUND

The rumbling sound became louder. Tag jumped up. It was coming from right beneath his feet inside the cage.

"More of Thorn's spies?" Skyla asked, her eyes wide.

Tag stepped back as the ground shook. Dirt started to sink into a small hole. It got bigger and bigger until half the ground had gone. Skyla clung to the bars of the cage.

RUMBLE! TUMBLE!

Tag and Skyla jumped as a small brown head popped up from the middle of the hole.

Two small, black eyes blinked at them. It was a mole.

"Hello!" the mole said, peering up at Tag. "I'm Monty. Are you Tag?"

Tag nodded slowly. He was so surprised he was unable to speak.

Monty smiled, then looked up at Skyla. "You must be Skyla," he said. He glanced around the cage. "But where is Blaze?" he asked. "She's supposed to be here, too."

Blaze gave a small peep from her cage.

"She's over there," Skyla said.

"How do you know our names?" Tag asked, finding his voice.

"No time to explain," Monty said. "More of Thorn's spies are on their way."

"Will you help us escape?" Tag asked.

"That's what I'm here for!" Monty grinned. "Moles are great diggers."

He disappeared back down the hole.

Seconds later, Blaze stamped at the ground in her cage as the dirt sunk into a deep hole, just as it had in Tag and Skyla's cage. She peeped as loudly as she could through her tied-up beak.

"It's okay, Blaze," Skyla called, letting go of the bars of the cage. "Monty is going to help us."

Just then, Monty's head popped up in Blaze's cage. "Hello!" he said.

Blaze stepped forward, but her feet slipped and she fell right into the hole, feet-first.

"Blaze!" Tag shouted. "Are you okay?"

"Tag!" Skyla shrieked behind him as she slipped on loose dirt and fell into the hole.

Tag peered into the deep, dark hole. There was no sign of Skyla, Blaze, or Monty. But he knew his friends had to be down there somewhere. In the dark forest, he could hear the marching sound. It sounded louder than ever. Even more spies had joined the army.

Tag took a deep breath and stepped to the edge of the hole. And jumped!

CHAPTER 10

IN THE TUNNELS

T ag fell for what felt like forever.
THUD!

He landed on cold, damp mud.

"Blaze?" Tag called. "Skyla?" The tunnel was dark. He couldn't see a thing.

"Tag!" Skyla replied. She was right next to him.

Tag hugged his friend, glad that she was okay. "Where is Blaze?"

Skyla scurried a little way ahead. "She's over here!" Skyla said. "We need to untie her."

They pulled at the webbing around Blaze's beak and wings until they came free.

"Peep!" Blaze called. "Peep, peep, peep!"

"We have to stay quiet," Tag whispered. "Blaze, can you light the way for us?"

There was a rustle of feathers. Slowly, the tunnel grew brighter as Blaze's feathers glowed.

Tag, Skyla, and Blaze walked through the tight, narrow tunnel, wondering what had happened to Monty.

"There you are!" a voice said behind them. "I'm afraid I got a little lost in the tunnels when I went back to fill in my holes—and to grab your weapons. Moles don't see too well, you see."

Monty handed Skyla and Tag their weapons.

"Thank you for helping us, Monty," Tag said. "But how did you know where we were?"

"I am a friend of Grey's," Monty told them. "He told me about your quest and about the Ember Stone, and he asked me to find you."

"Are you from Valor Wood?" Skyla asked.

"Moles and many other creatures used to live in *this* part of Perodia—before Thorn and The Shadow destroyed everything up there." Monty pointed aboveground. "But we moles still live underground here, and we use the tunnels to spy on Thorn."

"That sounds dangerous!" Skyla said.

"Thorn and his spies don't know about the tunnels," Monty said. "We fill in our holes so they never see them. You are safe down here. But we must hurry. We need to get you all to Valor Wood."

Skyla and Blaze followed after the little mole, but Tag paused. "Wait!" he said. "We can't leave without my sack."

Blaze pointed at Monty. "*That's* what I've been trying to tell you," she told Tag. "I saw the sack fall into a hole!"

Monty grinned as he pulled something out from behind him. It was Tag's sack. "As soon as I heard the wolves, I knew you were in trouble. So I tunneled up and grabbed your sack before Thorn's spies saw it."

"Thank you!" Tag said. He looked inside the sack. The Ember Stone was safe.

"Monty," he said as they continued on, "we saw prickle ants and crag beetles marching toward Valor Wood. And locusts and tiger bats filled the sky. When that horn sounded, the wolves ran off to join the march. Why are Thorn's spies all together in The Shadowlands now?"

"What is Thorn planning?" Skyla added.

"They are preparing for a battle," Monty said quietly. He stopped and turned to the friends. "They are preparing to attack Valor Wood."

CHAPTER 11

TO VALOR WOOD

The friends followed Monty through the maze of tunnels. Blaze's feathers lit the way, but the tunnels all looked the same. Wet, muddy, and dark.

I'm glad Monty is with us, Tag thought. *We would be lost down here without him.*

"I will take you to the edge of Valor Wood," Monty told them as they rushed on. "But I must stay in The Shadowlands to find out more about Thorn's plans."

"Thank you," Skyla replied. "You are doing important work."

"Hurry," Monty said. "Thorn will know that you have escaped by now. It won't be long until his army reaches Valor Wood. I've already sent word to Grey about Thorn's attack, so he can get ready. But you still need to find the last piece of the Ember Stone before the battle begins."

Tag moved as fast as his legs could carry him. He wished he and Blaze could fly. But the tunnel was too narrow.

"Almost there," Monty said, after they had continued on in silence. "You should be safe when you reach the surface. Grey told me how the Owls of Valor protect the forest."

"I've always wanted to be an Owl of Valor," Tag told Monty. "But I'm not sure I have done a good enough job protecting my friends to prove to Grey that I am ready. We would still be trapped in The Shadowlands if it weren't for you."

"It wasn't your fault we got caught, Tag," Skyla said.

"You will be an Owl of Valor one day," Blaze added.

Monty smiled at Tag. "Your friends are right," he said. "Grey has told me a lot about you—and about Skyla."

The friends started to walk upward through the tunnel. It felt like they were climbing a steep hill. Ahead, Tag could see an opening filled with bright light.

"This is where I must leave you," Monty said. "Just follow the light."

"Thank you, Monty," Tag said.

Blaze gave Monty a quick hug.

"Be careful," Skyla said.

"You too. Good luck!" Monty called as he scurried away, down into the dark tunnel.

Tag led the way toward the light. As he got closer, the light got brighter.

Tag knew he was back in Valor Wood before he reached the surface. He could smell the fresh leaves on the trees, and hear the trickle of the stream with its sweet water. Most of all, though, he felt it in his heart. A warm feeling spread through his feathers.

The three friends stepped out into the open air. Tag had to cover his eyes with his wing.

The warm sun shone down on them, and Tag smiled. They were home.

HOME

It had been a long time since Tag had been home, but he still remembered every path, every tree, and the way to Grey's tree.

"We need to find Grey," Tag said. "He'll know what to do next."

"We need to find the last piece of the Ember Stone first," Skyla argued.

"But we don't know where to look," Tag said. "That's why we need to find Grey."

Blaze nodded, and the friends hurried on.

Tag stopped suddenly and sniffed the air. Something was burning. Small puffs of smoke were coming from his sack. He reached inside, then—

"It's hot!" he cried, dropping the sack.

Blaze took out their piece of the Ember Stone. It was glowing bright purple and it was hot. Very hot.

"The last piece must be close by!" Skyla exclaimed, jumping in the air.

Blaze jumped up and down, too. Then she raced down a path through the trees.

"Blaze!" Tag called. "Wait for us."

"She must know where the last piece is!" Skyla shouted. She followed Blaze, leaping from tree to tree in the branches above.

The friends sped on until they reached a clearing with three large, creepy caves. The wind blew in and out of the caves, making a howling sound.

WOOOOOOOOOOOOOOOO!

"Tag!" Skyla cried, jumping down from her branch to land beside him and Blaze. "Those are the Howling Caves!"

Tag looked at Blaze. She stood in front of the mouth of the biggest cave, holding the Ember Stone in her beak. It glowed brighter than ever.

"This is where we found Blaze's egg," Tag said. "It's where our adventure began."

"Blaze," Skyla said, "is the last piece of the Ember Stone inside one of those caves?"

Blaze nodded.

"We should try the one where we found your egg, Blaze," Tag suggested.

"Last time we were here, the caves were filled with tiger bats," Skyla whispered. "Do you think there are still some in there?"

"They will be with Thorn's army now," Tag said as Blaze headed into the cave.

Tag and Skyla hoped there really were no spies inside. They followed Blaze into the mouth of the cave.

THE LAST PIECE

Tag and Skyla stayed close to Blaze. The Ember Stone's purple light filled the darkness. They walked deeper into the cave. It was quiet and empty.

Finally, Blaze stopped. The three friends could see a light a little way ahead. Another stone shone back at them!

Blaze put their piece on the ground. "The last piece," she said as she stepped toward the new stone.

Tag and Skyla watched as Blaze lifted the glowing stone from a narrow ledge inside the cave wall. She turned and placed the small stone beside their larger piece.

Then she stood back.

"We should stand back, too," Tag told Skyla, and they moved away.

The three friends watched as the two glowing stones began to wobble and shake faster and faster. A humming sound filled the cave. The sound was louder than ever before. Then, slowly, the stones moved closer to each other, sliding across the ground until—

"Cover your eyes!" Blaze shouted.

An explosion of bright, golden light filled the cave. Its warm blast almost knocked Tag and Skyla off their feet. Suddenly, Blaze's feathers lit up—one by one—until she looked like she was made of gold! Her feathers sparkled as brightly as the now-golden Ember Stone.

"The stone is complete!" Tag said. "We did it!"

"Woo-hoo!" Skyla cheered.

The three friends hugged and laughed. The Ember Stone's golden glow grew duller, and Blaze put it into Tag's sack.

"We must get this to Grey right away," Blaze said.

They were headed out of the cave when Skyla stopped.

"Look!" she said, pointing at the cave wall.

Tag took a closer look. There were two wall drawings of firehawks, just like the  drawings they had seen on Fire Island.

But these pictures were different. The first cave drawing showed the firehawks flying up into the clouds.

The second drawing was of one golden egg inside a cave.

Skyla looked at Blaze, then at Tag. "Do you think . . . ?" she whispered.

Tag knew what Skyla was thinking: The drawing was of Blaze's egg.

THE GOLDEN FEATHER

"Are you sure that is a drawing of *my* egg?" Blaze asked her friends.

"It makes sense. This is the same cave where we found your egg. And your egg was all alone, just like in that drawing," Tag said.

"Think about it," Skyla began. "The drawings on Fire Island showed what happened to the Ember Stone. What if these cave drawings show what happened to the firehawks?"

"But all they show are firehawks flying up into the clouds," Blaze said with a shrug. "That doesn't really tell us anything."

"We don't have time to think about this now. We need to find Grey," Skyla said. "Once we defeat Thorn, we can look at these pictures more closely."

The friends started walking back to the cave entrance.

Tag was worrying about what would happen when Thorn and his spies attacked Valor Wood.

"I hope Grey and the Owls of Valor are ready," Tag said. "Thorn has a big army."

"Yes, but we have the Ember Stone now," Blaze said.

Tag smiled at Blaze, and they hurried on.

"What's this?" Skyla said, squeezing her paw into a craggy opening in the wall.

She pulled out a long, sparkly, golden feather. She held it up to Blaze. "It's just like your feathers," she said.

She showed the feather to Blaze, then pulled another golden feather from beneath her armor. "And it's like this one we found near the drawings on Fire Island."

Ahead, at the entrance of the cave, the wind howled louder than ever.

WOOOOOOOOO!

Tag, Skyla, and Blaze stepped outside. Then—

CRASH!

Tag jumped as a huge crash of thunder echoed around the caves.

"Hurry!" Tag shouted over the booming sound. "The Shadow is getting closer."

GREY'S TREE

The sun wasn't as bright as it had been before. Dark gray puffs of clouds were moving across the sky.

"We should fly," Tag said. "It's the quickest way to reach camp."

"Okay. Just stay out of sight," Skyla agreed. "We need to be extra careful now that the Ember Stone is complete."

Tag and Blaze flew as fast as they could.

Finally, Tag spotted the center of the Owls of Valor's training camp. He could see the wooden huts, and the weapons laid out. There were silver swords, daggers, shields, and helmets.

Grey's tree stood in the center of camp. It was the oldest and tallest tree in Valor Wood.

Tag landed in front of the large door at the bottom of the tree trunk. He banged on it as hard as he could.

"Grey!" Tag called. "It's us. Tag and Skyla and Blaze."

Skyla looked around the camp. "Where is everyone?" she asked. Usually the camp was full of owls and other creatures. But now it was empty.

Tag lifted his wing to knock again, but the door quickly opened and he, Skyla, and Blaze were pulled inside. The door slammed shut behind them.

"Be quiet out there!" a loud voice boomed. It was Maximus, the captain of the Owls of Valor.

Tag had forgotten how loud Maximus was.

"Monty sent us a message that you would be here hours ago! Where have you been?" he boomed again.

"Never mind that, Maximus," another voice said from above.

The three
friends looked up.
Tag felt a rush of
happiness as Grey
flew down to
greet them.

"They are
here now," Grey
said, patting Tag
on the shoulder.
"That is all that
matters."

Together, they climbed the wooden steps
to the very top of the tree. Grey looked at
each of them in turn, giving them a big smile.
"You have the Ember Stone?" Grey asked.

Tag nodded. Blaze pulled the warm stone
out of Tag's sack. It was still glowing but not
as brightly as before.

"You have done well," Grey said.

"We have no time to lose," Maximus said. "Thorn's army has surrounded Valor Wood. This will not, however, only be a battle for Valor Wood. This will be the battle for *all* of Perodia. The Owls of Valor are preparing to fight, but even with the magical Ember Stone, Thorn could still defeat us."

"We will need help," Blaze said.

Grey smiled. "You have grown so big since I last saw you, Blaze."

Tag thought back to all the friends who had helped them along the way. "We could ask our *new* friends to help us," he suggested.

"But how will they know to come?" Skyla asked.

"Monty and the moles should be able to send them messages through the tunnels below Perodia," Tag said.

Grey nodded. "We will need everyone's help to win this battle."

GREY'S ARMY

"**P**erry!" Grey hooted out a window.

There was a rumble outside, and a mole popped up out of the earth. She hurried into Grey's tree.

"We need you and your friends to tunnel to different parts of Perodia," Grey told Perry. He lifted a wing at Tag to speak.

Tag nodded. "Please find Thaddeus and the spider monkeys at Fire Island, Coralie and the seals at the Crystal Caverns, the bears and grumblebees in the flower-filled meadow near the Whispering Oak, and Stanley the sloth at Lullaby Lake."

Maybe, Tag thought, *with our friends' help, we can save Perodia.*

"I'm on it!" Perry said, giving Tag a wink before she raced outside and back into her hole.

"What about Nova and the nixies?" Blaze asked.

Tag pulled out the magical shell Nova had given him. "The nixies live underwater," he said. "The moles can't reach them. We'll have to figure out how to use—"

TA-RAAAA! TA-RAAA!

Loud horns sounded. They called every creature in Valor Wood and beyond—to let them know to be ready to fight.

"Take Tag, Skyla, and Blaze to the clearing!" Grey told Maximus. "I'll meet you there."

The three friends felt hopeful as they rushed out of Grey's tree.

But when they stepped outside, the sky was even darker than before. The sun had disappeared behind thick, dark clouds, and a storm raged around them. Flashes of lightning filled the air, with big crashes of thunder that shook the ground.

"The Shadow is almost here!" Skyla shouted. "Our friends will never make it in time!"

Tag held Skyla's paw in one wing and Blaze's wing in the other. He looked at his friends. "We still have the Ember Stone," he said.

"And you have me," Blaze added.

Together, they raced to a large clearing.
Tag gasped. All the creatures from Valor
Wood were there. Owls and squirrels,
mice and rabbits, young and old. Holding
weapons and wearing armor. Ready for
battle. And there, right in the middle, stood
the fiercest, strongest warriors in all of
Perodia: the Owls of Valor.

Grey swooped down over their heads to land on a tree stump in the middle of the clearing.

Tag pulled out his dagger. Beside him, Skyla held up her slingshot, and Blaze's feathers glowed.

"We're ready," Grey said. "For the battle for Perodia."